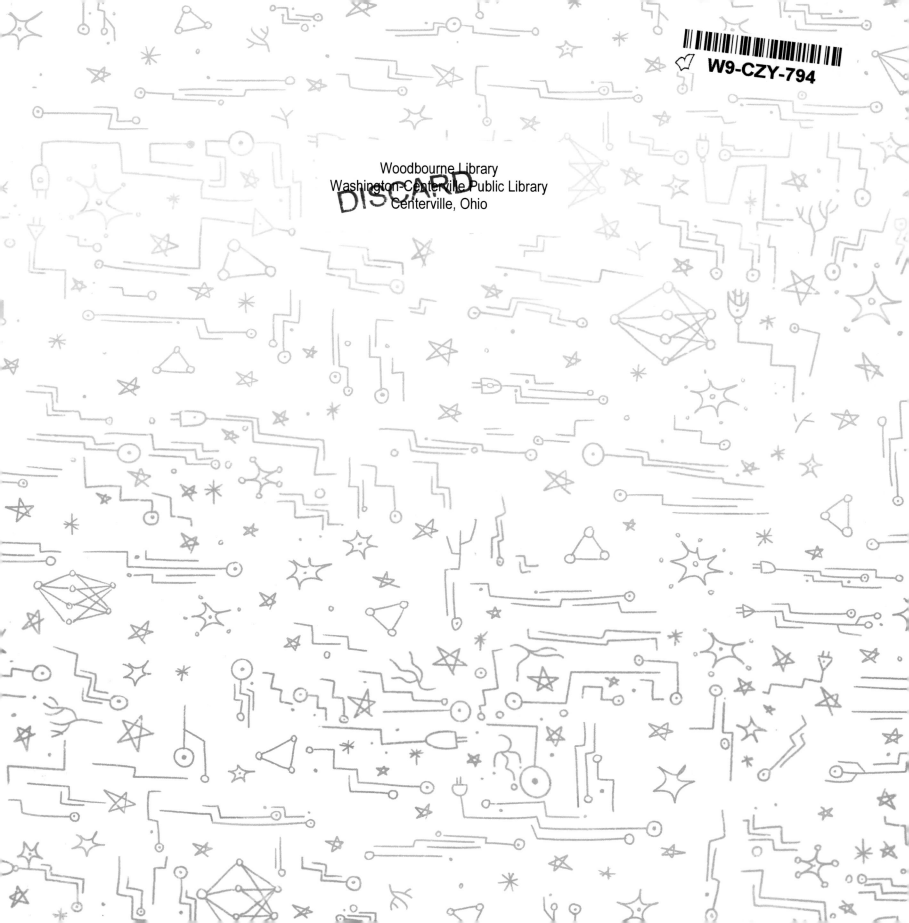

Praise for **Ara**

"We've always said, 'If she can see it, she can be it.' With this story, girls can see leaders and be inspired to become one. A book for all ages and genders!"

GEENA DAVIS, FOUNDER AND CHAIR OF GEENA DAVIS INSTITUTE ON GENDER IN MEDIA

"Ara and her friends are more than just characters; they are models for girls and boys to follow if they are curious about the world—and want to build a better one."

ERIC SCHMIDT, FORMER EXECUTIVE CHAIRMAN AND CEO OF GOOGLE

"Ara's story can inspire a whole new generation of girls to become engineers, coders, or computer scientists. Our world needs more girls like Ara."

HADI PARTOVI, CEO OF CODE.ORG

"Stories help us understand ourselves, each other, and the world around us. In a more and more technical world, we need stories like Ara's to help us bring up the next generation of problem solvers."

LINDA LIUKAS, AUTHOR OF *HELLO RUBY* SERIES

"The world needs more girls in tech, and curious, young Ara provides a delightful entry point. This book is a beautifully illustrated adventure highlighting diverse, real-life engineer role models sure to inspire future STEM stars."

DEBRA STERLING, CEO OF GOLDIEBLOX

"This book is beautifully drawn and supports a great cause! It is so important to encourage our young girls to become leaders in STEM fields—and this book does just that. A great bedtime story for any little engineer-to-be."

RACHEL IGNOTOFSKY, AUTHOR OF *WOMEN IN SCIENCE* AND *WOMEN IN SPORTS*

Ara
the Dream Innovator

by **Komal Singh**

illustrated by **Ipek Konak**

PAGE TWO
BOOKS

*In memory of my Naani HK and Aunties PK, SK, and MC,
who were dreamers, teamers, doers! —KS*

*To the memory of my beloved father, Rıdvan Konak,
who taught me how to build dreams and reality in cautious harmony. —IK*

Cataloguing in publication information is available from Library and Archives Canada.

ISBN 978-1-989603-59-8 (hardcover)

Page Two
www.pagetwo.com

Edited by Tiffany Stone
Copyedited by Rachel Ironstone
Layout and art direction by Teresa Bubela

Printed and bound in Canada by Friesens

Distributed in Canada by Raincoast Books
Distributed in the US and internationally by Publishers Group West, a division of Ingram

20 21 22 23   5 4 3 2 1

AdventuresOfAra.com

Dear parents and mentors,

I'm a techie by day and a storyteller mom by night—someone who likes innovations and ice creams, problem solving and pottery spinning.

After the success of *Ara the Star Engineer*, I embarked on a side project with a team of colleagues. In our spare time, we started a start-up to explore novel ways we could apply tech modalities to take kids' books beyond 2D to 3D and virtual reality, make them more accessible, and even transform characters using responsible AI so they look like underrepresented readers.

Starting-up took a whole lot of grit. I learned many new skills: how to feel comfortable putting myself out there, how to pitch my idea to crowds of strangers to get it funded, how to build a diverse team with equally diverse skills, and how to inspire my team to code and build things. Along the way, I met mentors who shared their experiences and cheered me on, helping me to face failure yet start again. All this while balancing my core work and, of course, two little droids of my own!

My adventure inspired me to write this book. Many studies show women founders of tech start-ups remain a startling minority. Most venture capital funding (big-time money) isn't directed towards women- and minority-owned companies. Such founders lack access to representative mentorship and networking that would allow them to scale up. By equalizing resources, opportunity, and mentorship, we could have a greater number of women-founded unicorn companies (billion-dollar successes), resulting in more equitable product innovation.

I hope this book gives children (and adults!) a peek into the amazing world of start-ups and the journey of innovation. That it inspires with its portrayal of underrepresented innovators and founders. That it highlights the importance of working with diverse people and including different perspectives. That it encourages us to take a chance on ourselves, to chase our big ideas. That it cultivates the courage to fail fast and start again. And that it serves, in its own small way, as a tool to help re-level the playing field for future founders.

Read together, learn, and wonder—start up and scale up your *inner innovator*!

Komal Singh

My TEDx Talk, "Recoding Stories," elaborates on my adventure.

Hello, World!

I am Ara, and this is my assistant, DeeDee.
I might be small, but I love to dream BIG.

"That's right, DeeDee. And since the best ideas come to me in my dreams, I invented this Dream Decoder. It captures those great ideas so I don't forget them when I wake up."

The Dream Decoder...

...parses dream signals...stores...sorts...indexes...searches...

...and plays back my coolest dreams.
"What if every kid had one?" I ask DeeDee. "Imagine how many great ideas we could capture and collect!"

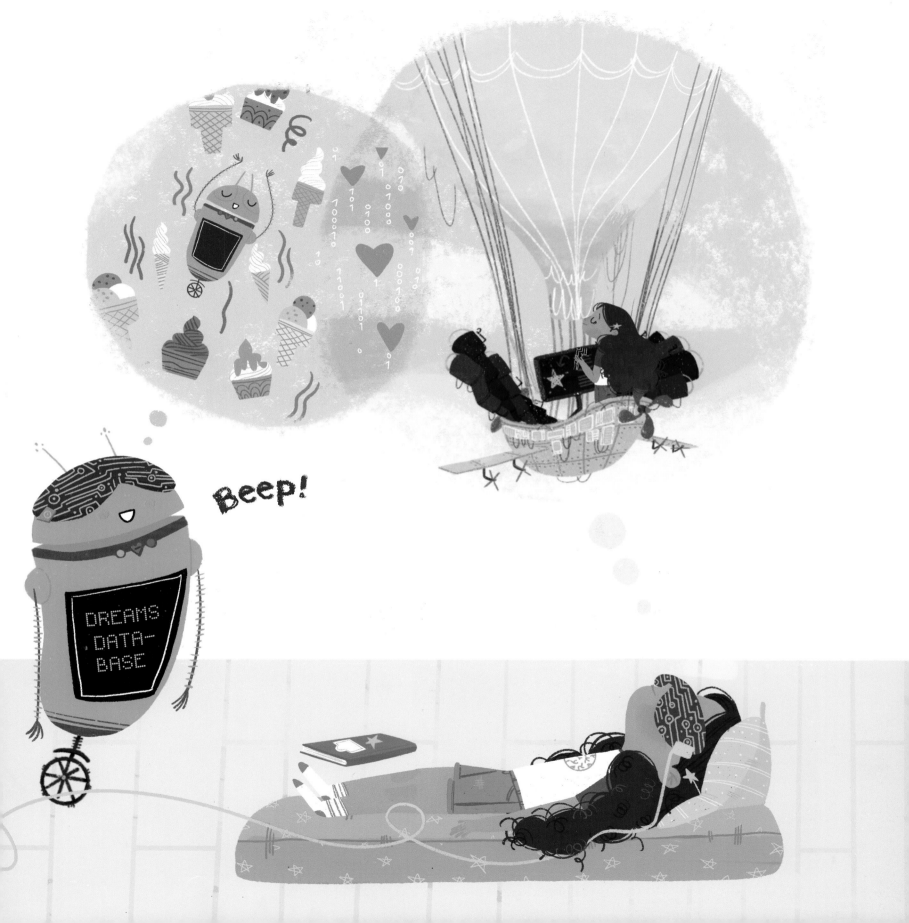

Beep!

DREAMS
DATA-
BASE

My grandma is an **Extraordinary Entrepreneur**. She builds awesome gadgets that make people's lives easy in fun ways. Naani overhears us and looks intrigued.

"Ara, my dear," says Naani, "you are a creator, an improver—a true **innovator**! You need your own **start-up**. Then you can build the Dream Decoder FTW: For The World!"

"That sounds amazing, Naani. But what's a start-up?" I ask, puzzled.

#1

BEST TEAM-WORK

TIPS LOADING

INNOVATOR'S
CHOICE

WoW
PATENT

"Think of it as a scrappy company, formed by friends who have a common passion to create something new, to solve a problem no one has dared to." She smiles and adds, "You can start a start-up and be its **founder**."

"Aha! I'm going to be an innovator *and* a founder!" I say excitedly.

"And, DeeDee, you'll be the best **co-founder**. We have a partnership of friendship."

Beep!

CO-
FOUNDER

"Every innovator begins with an idea," says Naani.
"But everyone's journey to bring that idea to life is unique.
I can't join you, but I've programmed DeeDee with some tips
to guide your adventures. Remember to do good things FTW."

"Alright, DeeDee,
how do we get started?"

Tip!

BOLD
MISSION

"That sounds cool! Naani had a great one:
'Good things FTW.'
What do you think, DeeDee?"

Beep!

FAMOUS!
TREATS!
WINS!

GOOD THINGS
FTW

"Okay, DeeDee, what next?"

"Aha, great tip! With a diverse team of many different kinds of people, we can come up with unique ways of thinking and working. Plus get lots done. Plus cheer each other on.

But, hmmm...where do we find this team?"

"Let's go to the **hackathon**!"

The hackathon is like a science fair—for innovators, SO many of us. We're all excited to team up and work on making our innovations even better. At the end, the most amazing innovation wins!

"Alright, DeeDee, we need to get people to join our team. But how?"

I'm really nervous to speak in front of such a huge crowd...

But then I remember the first time I told Naani about the Dream Decoder. She loved it. It's a great idea—FTW!

As I end my **pitch**, many people start applauding, eager to join our team!

We get going to make the Dream Decoder work for more kids than just me.

...refactor code...

...experiment...

...test...

...pivot...

It's finally time to pick the winner. A **Cool Connector** checks out our improved Dream Decoder. She loves bringing people together. If she picks us, we're sure to get even more help making the Dream Decoder FTW! Fingers (and antennae) crossed!

"Your invention is good and works well for many kids," says the Connector, "but not *all* of them. It needs to include everyone. I feel there's room to make it even better, even more **inclusive**. I'm afraid you are not the winner."

Oh no! Looks like our journey ends here. All of us Super Solvers feel so disappointed.

But then the Connector adds, "However, I see your passion. I'm willing to offer you a golden ticket to the **accelerator**, a place where you can improve your Dream Decoder even more. Are you up for the challenge?"

Our team gets excited, and we huddle to discuss.
It will be hard work. Can we do it?

We make our decision.
"Let's go to the accelerator!"
we cheer.

The accelerator is enormous! Each start-up has its own cool place to work. There are labs and makerspaces everywhere. And well-known kidnovators from around the world. We see many mentors helping the teams.

As we walk down the Hall of Founders, we see pictures of real-life superheroes, some whose start-ups went on to become **unicorns and narwhals**. These are cool names for big-time successes!

SEED & SERIES A, B, C FUNDING

① Family and friends round
② Seed round
③ Series A
④ Series B
⑤ Series C Onwards

TOP SECRET!

STEALTH MODE START-UP

2

We demonstrate our Dream Decoder.

But no one is super excited to offer us feedback or help us.
The whole team is discouraged.

DeeDee convinces someone
to take a look.
Wow, they're a **Dynamic Disruptor** whose big ideas
have caused big changes!

"Can you help us make
our Dream Decoder more
inclusive?" I ask.

Beep!
Beep!

POKE
PING

The Disruptor spends time analyzing and replies,
"Yes. Let's brainstorm!"

Aha!

Our team gets to work.

The Disruptor looks thrilled with the progress we've made. "I'm happy you have learned firsthand how being inclusive of all kids makes your Dream Decoder more powerful."

The Dream Decoder is finally ready
FTW!

Now, how do we get it to everyone?

An email arrives from a **Futuristic Funder**.

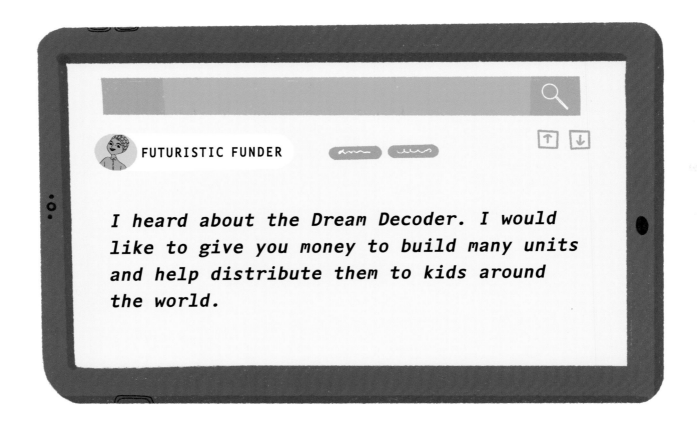

FUTURISTIC FUNDER

I heard about the Dream Decoder. I would like to give you money to build many units and help distribute them to kids around the world.

"Why would someone even do that?" I ask.

Beep!

ANGEL INVESTOR

I turn to the team. "Should we take the Funder's offer?"

Tip!

STAY TRUE TO MISSION

I decide to quiz the Funder, just to be sure. "Why do you want to help the Super Solvers?"

She sighs. "We all face disease, climate change, hunger, poverty. There are so many big problems."

Then she smiles. "But I'm hopeful. Your Dream Decoder in the hands of every kid would give us fresh new ideas to begin to solve these problems, for the world."

"Aha! That's exactly the mission of the Super Solvers. Good Things FTW!"

Our team huddles, and we decide to accept the Funder's offer. Time to scale up and go global!

Beep!

DEAL DONE

On our journey, from start-up to hiccup to **scale-up**,
I have discovered the Secret Sauce of Success:

INCLUSIVE INNOVATION FTW

Idea: solve with your original thinking

Include: solve for all kinds of
people everywhere

Innovate: solve to
improve solutions

Inspire: solve to make
the world better

ARA,
YOU ARE
A DREAM
INNOVATOR!

Aha!

Maybe I'll dream of my next project tonight.

HALL of FOUNDERS

Let me introduce you to some of the tech start-up superheroes who inspire us **Super Solvers**.

ENTREPRENEURS who take big risks and persist to turn their ideas into reality

CONNECTORS who have the special ability to link people up for help and support

DISRUPTORS who create truly innovative products and services

FUNDERS who help start-ups find the money and resources they need to get started

And MORE!

Accessibility Activist

First Black Woman Unicorn Founder

Indigenous Innovator

MAAYAN ZIV

Maayan is the founder of a mobile crowdsourcing platform that allows people to search for, rate, and discover businesses and experiences based on their level of accessibility.

JULIA COLLINS

Julia is the founder of a robotic food prep company that automates the making of pizza and another company that makes climate-friendly snacks.

MARY GOLDA ROSS

Mary was the first female Native American engineer and a founding member of a stealth group that worked on top secret projects related to space travel.

Tech Disruptor

HELEN GREINER

Helen is co-founder of a company that makes small robots to help people with everyday chores, including mopping and vacuuming.

Inspiring Mentor

HUDA IDREES

Huda is the founder of a company that allows people to request, collect, and manage their own health information digitally, all in one place.

Hispanic Trailblazer

ALEXANDRA ZATARAIN

Alexandra is co-founder of an innovative sleep technology company that develops smart products to "optimize sleep to perfection."

Inclusive Education Advocate

SANSKRITI DAWLE

Sanskriti is co-founder of a company focused on making education more inclusive for the visually impaired, creating the world's first device that lets children learn to type and read in braille all by themselves.

Angel Funder

ARLAN HAMILTON

Arlan is the only queer Black woman to build a venture capital firm—a company that provides money to start-ups—from scratch. The firm invests in companies led by underrepresented founders: women, people of color, and LGBTQIA2S+ individuals.

Young Entrepreneur

EMMA YANG

Emma is the teenage founder of an app that uses artificial intelligence–based facial recognition to help patients with Alzheimer's (a memory loss disease) recall events, recognize people, and stay connected with loved ones.

GLOSSARY

< innovator > someone who introduces new ideas, products, or methods, or brings improvements to existing ones.

< pitch > the opportunity to introduce your idea to people in a short amount of time (seconds to minutes) with the aim of getting them interested in helping you.

< start-up > a young company founded by one or more people to create a unique product or service. Typically, start-ups are founded on a small budget by friends who are building new technology and/or using existing technology in a new way.

< founder > a person who starts a company. If there is more than one founder, each person (or droid <beep!>) is called a **< co-founder >**. These terms are usually used about technology-oriented companies.

< scale-up > the next stage of evolution of a start-up, in which the company is expanding its product, team, outreach, funding, etc.

< unicorns and narwhals > start-up companies that have achieved unusually great success and are now valued very highly (at more than a billion dollars!).

< hackathon > an intensive event, usually lasting a few hours to a few days, during which many coders meet, present their ideas, and work in teams to solve common social or technical problems.

< accelerator > like a school for start-ups, typically lasting a few months, where teams are given training, mentorship, access to resources, and funds (money). Its aim is to help start-ups get better at building their products and to set them up for success.

< diverse > having many types and varieties. The Super Solvers team is diverse, its members being of various cultures, races, and genders, possessing a range of physical abilities, and more.

< inclusive > accepting and embracing everyone for who they are. Ara wants the Dream Decoder to be an inclusive innovation that works for all kinds of kids by accommodating their unique traits and needs.

> **Diversity** is like being invited to dinner.
> **Inclusion** is like being served your favorite meal.

Innovate
with Ara and the
Super Solvers
online at
AdventuresOfAra.com